SPACE PENGUINS

BLACK HOLE BATTLE!

For Lucy Hirst, the real Peabo's friend
~ **L A C**

For Lyzi ~ **J D**

STRIPES PUBLISHING
An imprint of Little Tiger Press
1 The Coda Centre, 189 Munster Road,
London SW6 6AW

A paperback original
First published in Great Britain in 2014

Text copyright © Lucy Courtenay, 2014
Illustrations copyright © James Davies, 2014
Cover illustration copyright © Antony Evans, 2014

ISBN: 978-1-84715-466-8

A CIP catalogue record for this book is available
from the British Library.

Printed and bound in the UK.

10 9 8 7 6 5 4 3 2 1

SPACE PENGUINS

BLACK HOLE BATTLE!

L A COURTENAY

ILLUSTRATED BY
JAMES DAVIES

Stripes

MEET THE
SPACE
PENGUINS...

CAPTAIN:
Captain T. Krill
Emperor penguin
Height: 1.10m
Looks: yellow ear patches and noble bearing
Likes: swordfish minus the sword
Lab tests: showed leadership qualities in fish challenge
Guaranteed to: keep calm in a crisis

FIRST MATE (ONCE UPON A TIME):
Beaky Wader, now known as Dark Wader
Once Emperor penguin, now part-robot
Height: 1.22m
Looks: shiny black armour and evil laugh
Likes: prawn pizzas and ruling the universe
Lab tests: cheated at every challenge
Guaranteed to: cause trouble

PILOT (WITH NO SENSE OF DIRECTION):

Rocky Waddle
Rockhopper penguin
Height: 45cm
Looks: long yellow eyebrows
Likes: mackerel ice cream
Lab tests: fastest slider
in toboggan challenge
Guaranteed to: speed through
an asteroid belt while reading
charts upside down

SECURITY OFFICER AND HEAD CHEF:

Fuzz Allgrin
Little Blue penguin
Height: 33cm
Looks: small with fuzzy blue
feathers
Likes: fish fingers in cream and
truffle sauce
Lab tests: showed creativity
and aggression in ice-carving
challenge
Guaranteed to: defend ship,
crew and kitchen with his life

SHIP'S ENGINEER:

Splash Gordon
King penguin
Height: 95cm
Looks: orange ears and chest
markings
Likes: squid
Lab tests: solved ice-cube
challenge in under four
seconds
Guaranteed to: fix anything

LOADING...

My circuits suddenly feel as fresh as Saturn's best socks. My networks work! My operating system is operating! I would jump for joy if I had legs. But I'm a computer, so I can't.

My name is ICEcube. I wasn't designed to be eaten by metal-munching space beasts. I was designed to speed the Space Penguins safely through the universe aboard their ship, the trusty *Tunafish*. By the time that hungry Flogisaur was finished with us in our last adventure, the *Tunafish* was little more than a pile of rusty fish bones. Our ship's engineer Splash Gordon was responsible for the Flogisaur in the first place, so he worked extra hard to repair what was left of me. He mended everything aboard with the metal the penguins collected from the planet Flogiston. Now all that's left is the tidying up. It could take a while.

Splash isn't the only one around here who's brilliant at his job.

Captain Krill is the bravest leader a team of Space Penguins could wish for. Zero gravity? More like *hero* gravity.

Rocky Waddle flies like an eagle with a stubby tail and long eyebrows. (Only when he's behind the controls of the *Tunafish*, of course. Everyone knows penguins can't fly by themselves.)

And with his cooking and his karate, Chief Security Officer Fuzz Allgrin is... What's the word I want? I'm not used to my new circuits yet.

Oh yes. Small.

Everything's new and shiny now. These things make computers happy. But I have one tiny problem.

The penguins picked up a piece of metal on Flogiston that's making me nervous. I am one hundred per cent certain that it's meganesium. Meganesium is the most explosive material in the cosmos. Just get it wet and BOOM! Splash picked up enough to destroy this whole ship. I've tried warning the penguins, but they can't hear me – my speech-converter chip hasn't been fixed yet.

I hope Splash hasn't mended this ship just to wreck it again.

CHAPTER ONE

TIDY UP TIME

The *Tunafish* was a mess. Piles of metal shavings and wire clippings lay on the floor. Crusty cloths, grimy goggles and smouldering soldering irons hung out of drawers. New saucepans stood in jumbled heaps. ICEcube was right. Splash's miraculous *Tunafish* makeover was going to take a LOT of tidying up.

In the middle of the chaos, the Space Penguins stood in a puzzled circle around a shiny red piece of metal on the table.

The metal was flat and round like a biscuit, and glimmered ominously.

"What is it?" Captain Krill asked.

"The strangest metal I've ever seen," said Splash. He wiped his oily forehead with an even oilier cloth. "I tried to melt it down to make a new handle for one of Fuzz's saucepans, but it wouldn't melt."

A tear of happiness rolled off Fuzz's beak. It landed on the table, dangerously close to the meganesium. "That's the nicest thing anyone's ever done for me," he said.

"But he *hasn't* done it, Fuzz," Captain Krill pointed out.

Two more tears. *Splosh. Splosh.*

"It's the thought that counts," Fuzz sniffed.

Splash shook his head. "I've heated it. I've cooled it. I've hit it with everything in my toolbox. I've stressed it and shaken it.

I've even bounced it. And it still looks the same as it did when we picked it up. I've never seen a metal like it."

Rocky admired his reflection in the meganesium's shiny red surface. "Maybe we could use it as a mirror," he suggested.

"I'll keep it in my toolbox," Splash decided. "It might come in useful in the engine room."

Lifting his belly, the Ship's Engineer opened the egg-shaped toolbox nestling on his feet and popped the circle of metal inside.

"Right," he said, looking around the messy flight deck. "Time to tidy up."

Rocky started whistling. Fuzz wiped his eyes and stared at the ceiling. Captain Krill studied his flippers.

"Any volunteers?" said Splash.

"I'm setting the flight coordinates," said Rocky. "Sorry."

"And I am making cosmic cod cupcakes." Fuzz picked up a brand-new cupcake tray from the floor and waddled into the kitchen.

"Sorry, Splash," said Captain Krill. "I have a lot of … captainy things to do today."

"Why am I the only one who clears up around here?" Splash demanded.

"It's your mess," Rocky said. "And you're the one who brought a metal-munching monster on board the ship in the first place."

"He has a point," Fuzz shouted from the kitchen. "Anyway, I never ask you to clean my oven."

"Perhaps you should invent a cleaning machine," Captain Krill suggested, patting his Ship's Engineer on the back.

Splash stomped off to fill up a bucket. As he dunked his mop in the soapy water, the water slopped over his feet. Luckily for the *Tunafish*, his toolbox was waterproof.

The intercom suddenly gave a high-pitched whistle. A squeaky voice crackled through the spaceship.

"Help!" it whispered. "Help us!"

"What's that?" Captain Krill asked in his most alert voice. "Did someone say something?"

Rocky twiddled a couple of dials on the control panel. "It was a message, Captain. But I just lost the frequency."

Captain Krill jabbed a button.

"ICEcube," he said, "can you adjust the frequency?"

"Don't expect an answer," Splash said, mopping the floor extra hard and sloshing water everywhere. "I haven't fitted ICEcube's new speech-converter chip yet. I won't manage it until the end of the day now, with all this clearing up to do."

The intercom squealed as the voice returned. It was a little squeakier, and a lot more scared.

"Help us!"

"I recognize that tune," said Captain Krill, at the sound of jolly music in the background. "It's 'Starstruck', by Veezli Measly!"

He sang a few lines, tapping his feet to the rhythm. "*Starstruck, bad luck, being hit by a star can really suck. Feet on fire, ears ablaze, dazzled by your burning gaze...*"

"Cheesy," said Splash.

Captain Krill stopped singing and

cleared his throat. "Any idea where the signal's coming from, Rocky?"

"I'm getting a faint reading from section V of the universe, Captain," said Rocky.

"Zoom in on that section," the Captain commanded.

Rocky turned another dial. The voice returned, but even fainter and more squeaky than before.

"Mutiny aboard the *Superduper Startrooper*! Save us! *Before the black hole gets us!*"

CHAPTER TWO

THE TROUBLE WITH MAPS

The *Tunafish* fell silent as the voice faded away.

"I've heard of the *Superduper Startrooper*," said Fuzz, popping his head out of the kitchen. "It's in my *Corking Cosmic Cruiseliners* annual."

He fetched the large book from his sleeping quarters to show the others.

"Well, well, whelk," said Captain Krill, as they stared at the pictures in Fuzz's book. "That's a very big ship."

"Look, there's a black swirl in the middle," said Rocky. "Is that a black hole?"

The penguins turned the map over with difficulty. The key was marked with thousands of tiny symbols.

"Star," read Captain Krill, following the key with his flipper. "Comet. Asteroid field. Footpath. Supernova. I have no idea how astronauts used maps like these in the old days… Aha! Black hole!"

The symbol for a black hole was indeed a black swirl. Captain Krill exchanged a triumphant high-flipper with Rocky.

They started folding up the map again. It proved a lot harder than unfolding it.

"Set the coordinates, Rocky," panted Captain Krill, as he tucked the crumpled map back under the pilot's chair some twenty minutes later. "There isn't another moment to lose!"

Rocky set the *Tunafish* to full cruising speed. With its brand-new thrusters, tail fin and booster engines, the fish-shaped ship was soon tearing through space like its gills were on fire.

Fuzz served up his cosmic cod cupcakes for tea and Splash finally set to work on ICEcube's speech-converter chip.

Captain Krill gazed out of the windscreen, thinking about the five hundred helpless passengers aboard the *Superduper Startrooper* and humming the chorus to "Starstruck".

He loved a good rescue mission.

Five hours and one unexpected asteroid belt later, the *Tunafish* drifted to a halt in a wide stretch of deep black space.

"We're here, Captain," said Rocky. He brushed his eyebrows out of his eyes.

"At least, I think we are. We'd better check that map thing again."

"Is ICEcube fixed?" Captain Krill asked Splash hopefully.

Splash wiped his forehead. "Yes, Captain. Give it a go."

"ICEcube?" said Captain Krill. "This is your Captain speaking. We need to know about an asteroid belt in section V."

"*Kore wa kinkyū jitaidearu*," said ICEcube.

"Sorry," said Splash, waddling over to ICEcube with his spanner. "I must have fitted a Japanese speech-converter chip by mistake. Give me another half hour and we'll be sorted."

"You'll have to do that later, Splash," the Captain sighed. "We need your help to unfold the map again."

Even with everyone helping, it took fifteen minutes to unfold the map.

"Ah!" Rocky stabbed at the map with his flipper. "There *is* an asteroid belt, but it's a lot closer to the black hole than I was expecting."

"Does that mean *we're* a lot closer to the black hole than you were expecting as well?" Splash checked.

"Yup," said Rocky.

"Cool conga eels!" said Fuzz. "Black holes don't scare ME."

The penguins peered out of the windscreen. Starlight seemed to curve around a big expanse of nothing directly in front of the *Tunafish*. The black hole was there all right, silent and deadly and very, very dark.

"Black holes *should* scare you, Fuzz," said Captain Krill. "The pull of gravity from a black hole is so strong that it crushes everything it touches. Even penguins."

"Not this penguin," said Fuzz. "Who wants the last cosmic cod cupcake?"

No one was hungry. Fuzz popped it in his beak. Splash went back to fixing ICEcube's voice chip.

A familiar-looking long, sharky spacecraft was floating a little way ahead of them.

"That must be the *Superduper Startrooper*," said Rocky.

"Have we had another message in the past five and a half hours, Rocky?" asked the Captain.

Rocky shook his head, making his eyebrows flap. "Not a winkle, Captain. I'll try them again if you like." He leaned towards the intercom. "*Superduper Startrooper*, this is the *Tunafish*. Does anyone read me?"

There was no answer.

Captain Krill studied the immense

spacecraft through the windscreen. "Poor souls," he said. "A mutinous crew turning against its Captain and taking over a spaceship is a terrible thing. Haddock knows what they have done with the passengers."

"Do you think we're too late?" said Fuzz.

Splash eyed the black hole. "Maybe we should go home."

Captain Krill frowned. "The Space Penguins have never left a rescue mission uncompleted." He pointed through the windscreen with one flipper. "There's a docking pod underneath the *Superduper Startrooper*'s belly. We'll board her that way. Everyone must put on their spacesuits. Oh, and take a weapon." He paused, then added grimly, "We don't know what we're going to find."

Rocky docked the *Tunafish* beneath the *Superduper Startrooper*. The penguins put on their suits and grabbed their weapons.

Splash twisted one last screw on ICEcube's casing and patted the computer. "See you later, calculator," he said.

"Warning!" ICEcube said, in English this time. "You are taking meganesium aboard the *Superduper Startrooper*. I repeat—"

But the airlock had already clicked shut.

CHAPTER THREE

THE SUPERDUPER STARTROOPER

Stepping aboard the *Superduper Startrooper* felt like stepping inside a luxuriously carpeted cloud. Apart from the low hum of the cruiseliner's thrusters, the ship was silent.

The Space Penguins clanked up the narrow flight of spiral stairs that led from the docking pod. Fuzz led the way, his belt bristling with stun guns, pulse pistols and zap-o-blasters.

"Come out, come out, wherever you

are!" Fuzz shouted.

"We're the only ones who can hear you, Fuzz," said Splash, turning down the volume on his helmet.

"And this isn't hide-and-beak," said Rocky, his flippers wrapped tightly around his bazooka blammer. "There are dangerous mutineers on board."

"COME OUT, WHEREVER YOU ARE!" Fuzz shouted, even louder.

The lights suddenly went off. Ghostly back-up lights flickered on, casting greenish shadows. The low hum of the cruiseliner's thrusters spluttered and died. Now it really *was* quiet.

The last time Captain Krill had felt a prickling sensation like this, he had just stepped on a sea urchin. There was something creepy about this ship. He didn't like it one bit.

At the top of the stairs was a long

corridor, stretching from left to right.
It turned sharply at the corners, so the
penguins couldn't see what lay ahead in
either direction.

"We need to find the flight deck and
start the thrusters again," said Splash,
looking around. "Or we'll drift into the
black hole."

The penguins tried to remember the
layout of the *Superduper Startrooper* from
Fuzz's annual.

"The docking pod was directly
underneath the ship's belly," said Captain
Krill thoughtfully. "So we must be in the
middle of the ship. If I remember rightly,
the *Superduper Startrooper*'s flight deck
is aft."

"Who's daft?" said Fuzz.

"Aft means the back of the ship,"
the Captain explained. He looked at
the corridor. "Those spiral stairs have

confused me. Is aft left or right?"

"Left," said Fuzz and Splash.

"Definitely right," said Rocky. "I can feel it in my flippers."

They turned left. Listening to Rocky's flippers was generally unwise.

A row of twelve silvery robots glided around the corner in front of them, moving in a line across the carpet.

"Ninja PENGUIN!" Fuzz squealed, and aimed his stun gun.

"Stop, Fuzz!" said Splash. "Stun guns don't work on robots."

"Greetings," Captain Krill said quickly, in case the robots were unfriendly. "We come in peace."

"Sorry about the stun gun thing," Rocky added. "That was a mistake."

As the robots drew nearer, the Captain relaxed. "There's nothing to worry about, crew. They're just cleaner robots," he said.

"Cleaner than what?" Rocky stared at the spotless carpet behind the robots, and their long, silvery arms with their nozzle attachments. The word HOOVERTRON was printed on the robots' bellies. "Oh, you mean *vacuum* cleaner robots! We should steal one for the *Tunafish*."

"What have I told you about stealing, Rocky?" said Captain Krill.

"Don't get caught?" Rocky replied.

Splash peered at the flashing circuit boards on the Hoovertrons. "They're running on some kind of remote-controlled program," he said.

"Can we ask them what happened?" said Captain Krill.

Splash shook his head as the Hoovertrons whirred past. "Their programming is too basic, Captain. They simply carry out orders."

The corridor began to widen, revealing long windows on the left that faced the great and terrible darkness of the black hole.

"How long do we have before the gravity from the black hole gets us?" Rocky asked, staring uneasily at the view.

"Forty-three minutes," said Splash. "Roughly speaking."

Captain Krill hitched up his spacesuit, which was feeling a little baggy. "Then we have to avoid the mutineers and find the flight deck as fast as we can."

After several minutes they reached an archway on their right, which led through to a vast central space. The walls were high, and intricately decorated with deep golden zigzags. A huge glass roof stretched over their heads.

"What a place!" said Rocky, admiring the great glass ceiling with its view of the stars. "Perfect for a holiday."

"That's the idea, you beaked banana," said Fuzz.

Splash waddled over to a selection of deck games that hung on a rack nearby – skittles, a big version of tic-tac-toe and a selection of toy crossbows. Three brightly coloured targets were set into the golden wall opposite. He took down a toy crossbow and examined it.

"High-pressure valve, foam arrows," he said.

Holding the crossbow up to his shoulder, Splash pulled the trigger. *Fing!* The arrow shot from the crossbow and stuck, point-first, right in the centre of the middle target.

"Penguin power!" said Fuzz, impressed.

Splash shrugged modestly. "I have an eye."

"I have two," Rocky pointed out, "but I can't shoot like that."

There was a large ice rink shaped like a shooting star to the left of the targets. Straight ahead, a sign marked VIEWING PLATFORM pointed at a tall, spiral staircase that twisted up towards the great glass roof.

"Can we try the ice rink next?" said Rocky.

"There's no time for fun and games," said Captain Krill. He gazed up the staircase. "We have a flight deck to find. Perhaps we can work out where aft is from the viewing platform."

At the top of the stairs, the penguins were surrounded by windows on all sides, offering a near-perfect view of section V of the universe. The black hole lurked ahead. It looked closer than before.

"We must be in the shark-fin bit of the ship," said Rocky with a whistle. "You can see everything!"

From up on the platform they could see that the central deck below was divided into different sections. As well as the games and the ice rink, there was a library, a space garden, a climbing wall, a beauty parlour and a gigantic aquarium filled with colourful fish. Near the aquarium was a set of big golden doors.

Captain Krill studied the shape of the transparent fin curving over their heads. "The fin curves *behind* us," he said. He looked over the edge of the viewing platform again. "So those golden doors must be aft. Head that way, and we'll find the flight deck."

"Excellent detective work, Captain," said Splash.

Fuzz suddenly gasped and pointed.

"What the whale-blubber is THAT?" he said.

CHAPTER FOUR

FUZZ GOES FISHING

Far below the penguins, books lay scattered across the library floor. A host of Hoovertrons were collecting them up and placing them on to shelves. The books that remained spelled out something across the carpet.

"Someone's left a message!" said Captain Krill.

"But what does 'elps' mean?" said Fuzz.

"Perhaps it's like yelps," said Rocky. "Only quieter."

"Look! There are more letters in the aquarium, Captain," said Splash.

A long, eel-like robot was swimming around the aquarium, tidying up the rocks and pebbles that lay on the bottom. The largest rocks still spelled HE P U.

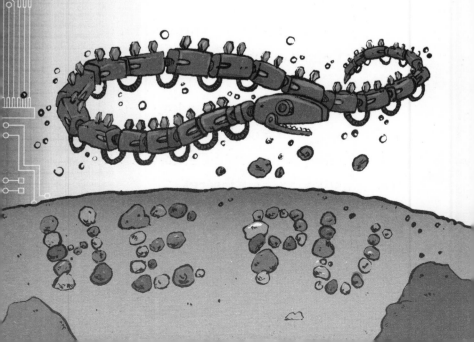

"They've spelled hippo wrong," said Rocky.

"This is all very fishy," said Captain Krill.

Fuzz's stomach rumbled. "What?" he said, when the others looked at him. "I'm looking at fish, you mentioned fish... I'm a penguin. I get hungry."

"Both messages are the same," said Splash. "The Hoovertrons have just tidied up different letters. If we put them together..."

"They say HELP US!" shouted Fuzz.

"Technically, they say HEELPP US," said Splash.

"It sounds extra urgent when you spell it like that," said Rocky.

"Quickly, crew," said Captain Krill. "We must get to that library!"

The penguins hurried back down the stairs. A bit too fast.

"Whoa!" Splash flapped his flippers, startled, as his feet got tangled in his oddly baggy spacesuit. He tumbled forward, taking Rocky with him, then Fuzz – and then the Captain himself.

WHUMP! CRUMP! FLUMP!

Within moments, the Space Penguins lay in a crumpled heap at the bottom of the stairs.

"I didn't mean *that* quickly," said Captain Krill.

By the time they waddled breathlessly into the library, the Hoovertrons had gone and the books were sitting neatly back on the shelves. There was no sign at all that a message had been left.

"Those Hoovertrons are too efficient," Fuzz complained.

"Not *that* efficient," said Splash.

Someone had spilled a cup of what looked like coffee on the golden carpet. Four wet footprints led from the brown puddle towards the exit.

Captain Krill clasped his flippers behind his back. "It's clear to me that four different-sized, one-legged aliens have recently been in this library," he said.

"How do you know that?" said Rocky.

"The coffee is still wet," the Captain replied. "And if you look closely at the footprints, they are all different sizes. Four aliens. One leg each."

His headset fizzed and crackled. "The suit's fine. A little stretched, maybe."

"Funny, my spacesuit feels a bit baggy too," said Rocky.

"Get out of that suit before you electrocute yourself on the circuitry, Fuzz," Captain Krill ordered. "Splash, what's the atmosphere like on board this ship?"

Splash pulled a winking electronic instrument out of his toolbox and took a reading. "Oxygen, Captain," he reported. "Safe to breathe."

The penguins all flipped open their helmets and took off their spacesuits.

"That's better," said Captain Krill, flexing his flippers. "My diet and exercise plan is clearly working because my suit was feeling strangely large. I'll have to adjust it when we get back to the ship."

"Hmm," said Splash, staring thoughtfully at the Captain's suit.

The eel's teeth glinted as it snapped its jaws at Fuzz.

"OW!" Fuzz roared, waggling his flipper. "It just BIT me!"

"Throw it back, Fuzz," said Captain Krill. "You don't know where it's been."

Moving around the *Superduper Startrooper* was much easier without their baggy suits on. The penguins left them in a heap by the aquarium. Splash tucked his toolbox among the suits too. It was getting strangely heavy.

More Hoovertrons appeared as the penguins reached the far side of the aquarium bridge.

"These guys look bigger than the other ones," said Rocky. "Hey, watch where you're going, scampi-chops!" he added, rubbing one vacuumed foot as the Hoovertrons whirred past.

Everything looked bigger on this side of the aquarium. The golden doors they'd seen from the viewing platform. The golden zigzag patterns cut deep into the walls.

"Can spaceships grow?" asked Fuzz. He studied his flippers hopefully. "Maybe I'll grow, too."

"Could the black hole be affecting the size of the ship?" Captain Krill asked Splash.

Splash was looking at the zigzag patterns on the walls with an odd look on his face. "Black holes can't change ships," he told the Captain. "But they can change organic matter. Living things. Penguins, for example. I don't want to worry you, but I'm starting to think—"

"Shh!" Captain Krill interrupted, holding up a flipper. "Can you hear that?"

A rhythmic sound vibrated through the penguins' bodies. It was coming from the other side of the large golden doors.

"It's that song again," said Rocky. "The one you like, Captain."

The Captain's face brightened. "'Starstruck'! We heard it in the background of that distress call, didn't we? The passengers must be in here! *Starstruck, bad luck, being hit by a star can really suck...*"

"We're looking for the flight deck, not the passengers, Captain," said Fuzz. He pointed away from the doors. "We should be going that way."

But drawn by the sound of his favourite song, the Captain had already leaned his flippers against the doors and pushed them open.

CHAPTER FIVE

COLD SOUP

A huge ballroom hung with three giant chandeliers met the penguins' eyes. The chandeliers were covered in hundreds of brightly blazing candles, which cast a warm yellow glow over an extravagant-looking banquet laid out on a long white table near the door.

"Those candles are a fire hazard," said Captain Krill, humming along to "Starstruck", as the tune poured from a set of speakers near the wall.

"But very pretty," said Rocky. "Useful, too, now the main lights have all gone out."

A number of smaller tables, brightly decorated with big pink helium balloons and flowers were positioned around a shiny gold dance floor. Bowls of pale green soup filled with floating ice cubes sat untouched at every place setting. The only thing missing from the richly decorated room was the party guests.

"No passengers," said Rocky, looking around. "Can we go and find those engines now, Captain? Er, Captain?"

Captain Krill was swaying to "Starstruck", his flippers clasped in front of him.

"*Feet on fire, ears ablaze, dazzled by your burning gaze,*" he sang. "In a minute, Rocky, this is my favourite part."

"That must be the robot chef Marin-8's

legendary galactic gazpacho!" said Fuzz, staring at the bowls of soup on the tables.

"You know, this tune isn't so bad the second time," said Rocky. He started dancing until his eyebrows twirled around his head.

"It wasn't bad the first time, either," said the Captain, feeling offended. "Did you know Veezli Measly wrote this after he was hit by a meteorite?"

Fuzz whooped and did a funky knee-slide. FLUMP.

"I was hoping to slide under you and out the other side, Captain," said Fuzz in a muffled voice, wedged somewhere underneath Captain Krill's tummy. "That's how it works in movies."

"It's not a dance move best suited to penguins, Fuzz," said the Captain, helping the little penguin to his feet.

"Wake up, you goofy guppies!" Splash snapped. "We have approximately twenty-one minutes to find the flight deck, switch the thrusters back on and get out of here before the black hole sucks us away like bathwater down a plughole! And to add to our problems, I think we're—"

The doors suddenly banged open.

"Weapons, team!" cried the Captain, reaching for his zap-o-blaster. His flippers met thin air.

"We left our weapons beside the aquarium with our spacesuits!" gasped

Rocky. "We'll have to rely on our wits!"

"You won't last long then, will you?" Fuzz said.

An army of fifty Hoovertrons whirred into the ballroom, heading towards the beautifully laid tables. They seemed more menacing than before, their hungry vacuum attachments sweeping around the room. Decorations, cutlery, glasses, tablecloths, balloons, galactic gazpacho. Everything started disappearing through the Hoovertrons' tubes, the pink helium balloons popping like gunfire.

SCHLOOP. CRUNCH. SCHLOOP. SQUEAK-POP.

"This is a whole new level of cleaning," said Fuzz, as the tables themselves started disappearing into the vacuum tubes. "Haven't these guys ever heard of recycling?"

Five tables had already disappeared. Now ten. Fifteen. The Hoovertrons were getting closer and closer to the penguins all the time, arms sweeping, sucking, crunching.

CRUNCH. SCHLOOP. CRUNCH. SQUEAK-POP.

"We need to get out of here," Captain Krill said. "I think these guys might be our mutineers!"

SCHLOOP. SCHLOOP. SCHLOOP.

"But they're running on too simple a program," Splash pointed out. "They can't think for themselves. So—"

"—someone else must be thinking for them!" Rocky finished. "But who?"

The big silver robots were everywhere, sucking and chomping and splintering the beautiful tables into nothing. The penguins looked helplessly towards the ballroom doors. They were further away than they had been expecting.

SCHLOOP. CRUNCH.

The penguins were completely surrounded!

CHAPTER SIX

ROBOT REVOLUTION

"I've got it!" Splash said, as the shredded remains of a pink helium balloon disappeared up the nose of a Hoovertron. "We'll fly out of here."

A Hoovertron's sucking arm swept dangerously close to Rocky's eyebrows, nearly tugging them from his head. "I hate to point this out at such a critical time, Splash," he shouted over the noise, "but PENGUINS CAN'T FLY."

Splash pointed at a nearby helium

balloon, still attached to its table. "Pull a ribbon loose and hold on to one of those!"

"Don't be absurd," said the Captain. "We're far too big to ride on balloons."

"That's what I've been trying to tell you, Captain," said Splash. "We're shr—"

SQUEAK-POP. SQUEAK-POP.

Balloons were exploding all around the room, as they shot up the vacuuming arms of the Hoovertrons.

"We are the Space Penguins!" Fuzz roared. "Watch us FLY!"

The little penguin scrambled up on to the nearest chair, but fell off again before he reached the seat. Captain Krill gave him a flipper-up, then heaved himself up as well.

The balloon ribbons were tied to a weighted block in the centre of the table. *When did the helium balloons get so big?* Captain Krill wondered, as he breathlessly unlooped the ribbons.

When did everything *get so big?*

"Lift-off!" cried Rocky, the first to wrap his balloon ribbon around his waist and float towards the ceiling.

Fuzz was next, then Splash. Captain Krill kicked with his legs, trying to swim through the air and catch up.

The Hoovertrons suddenly stopped what they were doing. The floating penguins gazed down from their helium balloons, wondering what had changed.

"Who's the red dude?" said Rocky, pointing.

A shiny, bright red robot had appeared through a door at the back of the ballroom. He was considerably bigger than the Hoovertrons, and wearing a tall white chef's hat. Buttons winked on his belly. Instead of hands, kitchen utensils – spatulas, whisks, cleavers and graters – hung at the ends of his four arms.

"Oh my codfish," Fuzz gasped. "That's Marin-8. The *Superduper Startrooper*'s robot chef!"

Marin-8's eyes shone with a weird brightness. His utensil-hands shook and clattered by his side.

"CLEAN," he ordered in a harsh metallic voice. "TIDY. CLEAN."

"Marin-8 doesn't look very happy," said Splash. "There's smoke coming out of his head."

"I feel like that sometimes," said Fuzz. "When you guys don't eat what I've cooked." He gasped for the second time. "The galactic gazpacho! How many tables were down there? Before the Hoovertrons sucked them up?"

"Fifty?" Captain Krill guessed.

"Fifty tables with ten place settings at each!" Fuzz said. "Five hundred plates of uneaten galactic gazpacho! Do you realize what this means?"

"You're good at maths?" Rocky suggested.

"It means *no one liked his soup*. No wonder Marin-8's cracking up!"

The penguins' balloons were starting to lose height. The penguins steered towards the long table – the only table the Hoovertrons had left untouched – and landed on the white tablecloth beside a vast flower arrangement.

Fuzz seized the opportunity to dip a flipper into a large bowl of galactic gazpacho and taste it.

"Yuck," he said. "Too much salt. No wonder no one ate it."

"Flowers grow big around here, don't they?" said Captain Krill, staring up at the waxy red undersides of three extremely large petals.

"They're not big," said a squeaky voice nearby. "You're small."

CHAPTER SEVEN

YOU SENT THE MESSAGE

Two strange-looking aliens crept out of the flower arrangement in front of the penguins. They were brown, with fins on their heads, very long arms and very short legs. The taller one was the same size as Fuzz.

"I'm NOT small," said Fuzz in a dangerous voice.

The bigger of the finned aliens pointed at himself. "I'm not usually this size. Nor is my wife. It's the black hole that's doing it."

"I've been trying to tell you, Captain," Splash sighed. "But you wouldn't listen."

The truth suddenly hit Captain Krill like a fish-shaped cricket bat. He clapped a flipper to his forehead. Now everything made sense. The spacious spacesuits … the massive menacing Hoovertrons … the huge pink helium balloons…

The footprints in the library didn't belong to four different-sized, one-legged aliens, but one shrinking alien, just as

Splash had suggested. And the penguins were shrinking too!

"We're Peabo and Peabo," said the bigger alien. "From the planet Peabo."

Rocky looked from one alien to the other. "Which is which?"

"I'm Peabo," said both aliens, helpfully.

"I am Captain Krill of the *Tunafish*," said the Captain. "And this is my crew – Rocky Waddle, Splash Gordon, Fuzz Allgrin."

"I am NOT SMALL," Fuzz repeated.

"So the black hole is shrinking us?" Rocky said.

"Finally," Splash said. "The ice cube drops."

"The black hole has affected every living thing on board the ship," said the smaller alien. "Peabos like us. Oomthrods and Warples and Ullabullas and Jimjams."

Rocky peered among the flowers. "Where is everyone else?"

"We escaped when Marin-8 took control of the ship," said the bigger Peabo. "The other passengers shrank more quickly than we did and were easy for Marin-8 and the Hoovertrons to round up. They're all locked in a cupboard in the library."

"The *chef* drove the ship into a black hole right in the middle of his banquet? Why?"

"No one liked his soup," said the smaller Peabo.

Fuzz looked meaningfully at the other penguins. "See what can happen when you upset a chef?"

"He went mad," said the bigger Peabo. "He's controlling the ship now and the robot staff are his army. They turned off all the lights and the engines. The black hole will swallow us all up unless you do something!"

"YOU sent the message! YOU left the words in the library and the aquarium!" said Captain Krill.

Peabo and Peabo brightened. "You saw our messages? We were worried in case the Hoovertrons tidied them away."

As if hearing their name, the Hoovertrons came to life again with a sudden whirring noise. Hundreds of robot eyes glowed in the penguins' direction. In the middle, Marin-8's eyes glowed the brightest of all.

"TIDY," he grated. "CLEAN. DESTROY."

"Time to leave," said Splash.

"If we can," said Rocky.

"Hey, Marin-8!" Fuzz shouted at the robot chef. "Your galactic gazpacho sucks!"

Marin-8's head started spinning.

"What did you say that for?" gasped Rocky. "Now he's *really* mad!"

"It's important to be honest about food," said Fuzz.

Captain Krill eyed the nearest balloon. He studied the burning candles on the chandelier. He made a decision.

"We're small enough to all ride one balloon now, including the Peabos," he said. "We must steer it towards that chandelier."

"But won't the balloon catch fire?" said Rocky.

"Yes!" said Splash, his eyes brightening as he saw the Captain's plan. "The balloon will burst." He pointed at the doors. "And we'll rocket through those doors, and away from Marin-8 and his Hoovertrons. We're almost at the aft of the ship. We'll be at the flight deck in two shakes of a dolphin's tail. Right, Captain?"

"Exactly," said Captain Krill. "It's an excellent plan," he added modestly, "even if I say so myself."

"Except the engine room and flight deck are fore," said one of the Peabos. "At the front of the ship. Past the ice rink and the games area."

There was a nasty silence.

"Ah," said Captain Krill.

"So we have to go back the way we just came?" said Fuzz.

"It seems so," said Splash.

"I *knew* we should have turned right," said Rocky.

"Captain? We have seven minutes," said Splash. "Give or take thirteen seconds."

The best captains always keep their heads in a crisis. "Plenty of time," Captain Krill said with a deep breath. "We will leave this ballroom as planned, and retrace our steps. Then we will power the *Superduper Startrooper* out of trouble and everyone can go back to normal size again. One for all..."

"And all for FISH!"

The Space Penguins and the Peabos grabbed on to the ribbon of the helium balloon.

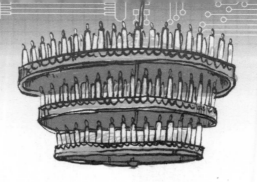

Marin-8's mad eyes gleamed even brighter as Fuzz untied the ribbon. Lights flashed on his belly.

Suddenly there was a fierce gust of air. The balloon blew wildly from side to side, nearly throwing off its passengers.

"Marin-8 must be controlling the central power system by remote!" Splash shouted, fighting to hold on as the balloon rose towards the chandelier. "He just turned the air-conditioning on!"

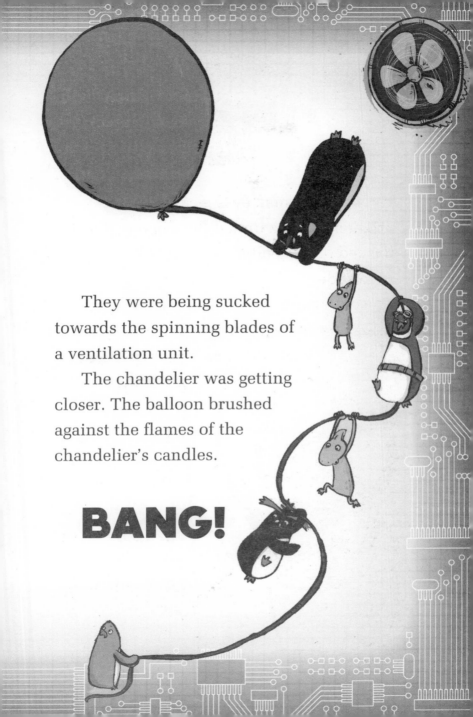

They were being sucked towards the spinning blades of a ventilation unit.

The chandelier was getting closer. The balloon brushed against the flames of the chandelier's candles.

BANG!

CHAPTER EIGHT

WHAT A RIDE!

The Peabos squealed again. The burst balloon rocketed towards the door so fast that the Space Penguins almost lost their flippers. The Hoovertrons and Marin-8 were a blur below them.

"We're going to crash-land!" Rocky bellowed, as they hurtled through the doors.

Captain Krill placed his flippers over his head in the way NASA had taught them.

"It's OK!" said Fuzz suddenly. "We're going to land in the—"

SPLOSH! SPLOSH, SPLOSH, SPLOSH!

Of all the places to land, a gigantic aquarium wasn't bad. The penguins went into swim-mode, angling their flippers, paddling hard with their feet and pointing their beaks like arrows.

"Swim ya laters, fat potaters!" shouted Fuzz, darting in and out of the water.

The Peabos had grown bright red gills and were swimming almost as fast as the penguins.

Rocky spun round in a watery arc to chomp up a fish. "I hope that guy agrees with me," he said, leaping from the water with a burp.

"It's too late to argue with it, Rocky," said Splash. "You've eaten it."

"Agrees with my TUMMY," explained Rocky, and burped again.

A huge, eel-like monster suddenly loomed through the water. Its metallic scales flashed and sparkled. Its vicious teeth shone like daggers.

"What in the name of narwhals is that?" said Captain Krill in shock, popping up to the surface.

"It's the guy I caught earlier!" said Fuzz. "I recognize those teeth."

"Keep swimming!" the Captain ordered, bursting to the surface to take another breath. "Don't let the fish get you!"

"An interesting problem," said Splash, skimming beside the Captain. "Seeing how fish are normally scared of *us*."

They dived back under the water again, swimming for their lives. The eel was getting closer.

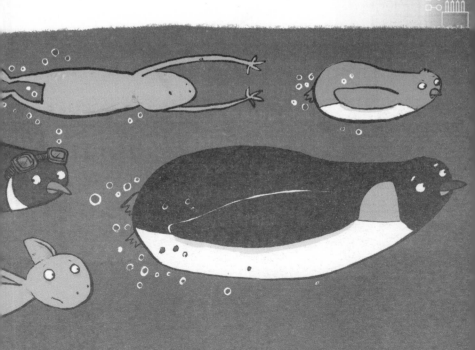

"How come it hasn't shrunk?" Rocky asked, the next time the penguins came up to breathe.

"Didn't we see an eel-like robot cleaning the tank when we were on the viewing platform?" said Splash. "I think you caught the only non-fish in the aquarium, Fuzz."

"If I can't eat it," said Fuzz, "I'll fight it instead. Ninja PENGUIN!"

Changing direction in the water, Fuzz swam straight at the metallic monster.

"He's too small to fight that thing alone," said Captain Krill.

"I'M NOT SMALL!" Fuzz shouted, as the robot eel whacked him right out of the water with its tail. "Chocks away, manta ray!"

The others dived after Fuzz, to lend him a flipper. As the robot eel gave another furious flick of its tail, the space mates soared through the air together.

They crashed into the corridor wall
and instantly started sliding.

"Whoa," shouted Rocky, trying to keep
his flippers by his sides, as they whooshed
along a golden ledge. They had lost the
Peabos somehow.

"Where are we?" shouted Splash.

"Who cares!" Fuzz roared, whizzing
faster than the others. "We're moving
in the right direction, and we're doing
it in style!"

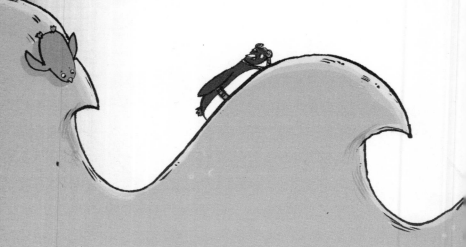

The golden ledge was climbing.
A precipice was looming…

"Whaa!" screamed Rocky, as they
sailed off the end.

WHAM!

The penguins landed hard on another
golden ledge and the whole thing started
again.

"We're riding the zigzags on the wall!"
Splash shouted, careening along beside
Rocky. "I love it!"

Each zigzag was bringing them closer to the carpeted floor of the cruiseliner. When they shot off the last zig, they tumbled head over flippers on to the floor. They had travelled past the viewing-platform steps and the library. The huge shooting-star shaped ice rink now glittered in front of them. Way beyond the rink and the games area, a long carpeted corridor ended at a door.

"That must be the flight deck," Splash said.

There was still a long way to go, and they had barely five minutes left.

"Cross the ice as fast as you can!" the Captain ordered.

The ice felt cold and comforting on their bellies. Fuzz and Splash zoomed beside the Captain, as Rocky whizzed along on his back. But it was still a long way for tiny flippers. Panting, the penguins crawled off the rink and flopped into the games area.

Whirr. Whirr. Whirr.

"CLEAN," came Marin-8's voice. "TIDY. DESTROY."

"Marin-8 and his metal army are about to cross the aquarium bridge," Captain Krill warned the others.

"Four minutes to go," Rocky moaned.

"Galloping goujons," said Splash suddenly, as he eyed the shiny, bright red robot. "The red metal in my toolbox, I've just realized what it is!"

"That's terrific and everything," said Rocky, giving Splash an urgent shove, "but we have to waddle down a massive corridor to save everyone's lives just now. Can we hear the science lecture later?"

"It's meganesium!" said Splash.

The penguins swung their heads sharply back to where their abandoned spacesuits lay in a heap beside the aquarium. Splash's toolbox was there, its eggy shape peeping out from underneath the suits.

"Meganesium?" said Captain Krill. "The most explosive metal in the universe?"

"All it needs is a drop of water, and BOOM," said Splash, "it would wreck this central space completely."

"Wouldn't it destroy the whole ship?" Captain Krill asked.

"Not quite," said Splash. "There isn't enough of it to breach the hull."

Captain Krill eyed the toy crossbow lying sideways on the carpet nearby. Now they were so small, the crossbow was the size of a cannon.

"Can you load that, Fuzz?" he said.

"On it," said Fuzz at once. "Rocky, lend me a flipper."

"What's the plan, Captain?" said Splash, as Rocky and Fuzz heaved a massive foam bullet into the crossbow chamber.

"We aim this toy weapon at your toolbox," Captain Krill said. "If we can burst it open and knock it into the aquarium, the magnesium will get wet and explode, taking those robots with it."

"Cool catfish," said Fuzz.

The trigger was so big it needed both Rocky and Splash to pull it.

"Fire!" cried the Captain.

Fing! The foam bullet made a quiet whizzing noise and nose-dived into the carpet a few metres from the toolbox.

Whirr. Whirr. Whirr.

"CLEAN. TIDY. DESTROY," said Marin-8, leading his Hoovertrons over the bridge.

"Again!" Captain Krill shouted.

Fuzz and Rocky fitted another foam bullet. Splash made a couple of adjustments. Once more the penguins heaved on the trigger.

Fing!

The foam bullet flew straight at the heap of spacesuits. Splash's toolbox rocked on to its egg-shaped tip, rolled over, broke open – and splashed into the aquarium.

CHAPTER NINE

THE FINAL SHOWDOWN

BOOOOOOOOOOOOOOOOOOM!!!!

Water, fish, glass, metal and robots cascaded into the air. The viewing-platform steps crashed to the ground, the ice rink cracked from side to side and the climbing wall fell into what was left of the aquarium. Water washed through the ship as the *Superduper Startrooper* rocked and shook like a shrimp in a tumbledryer – but the vessel stayed intact.

The dust began to clear. The penguins

cheered as heaps of robot springs, coils,
nuts, bolts, wires and rivets settled into
clinking piles.

A couple of Hoovertrons that had
avoided the explosion were madly
vacuuming up the mess. A few others
had made it as far as the ice rink, but
were now spinning round in confused
circles on the slippery surface.

"That's a *lot* of spare parts," said Splash happily.

"Look out, Captain!" said Rocky.

Marin-8 had survived the explosion – but only just. Water gushed from his articulated joints. He had only one utensil-arm left. Springs hung out of his belly and his chef's hat was tipped to one side. "CLEAN. TIDY. DESTRUG," he said in a watery, broken voice. "DESTRUG! DESTRUG!"

"I don't know which I prefer, destroy or destrug," said Rocky.

Captain Krill suddenly climbed into the crossbow chamber. "Turn this round and aim me at the flight deck," he said.

"You'll end up as penguin pâté!" Splash gasped.

"Can you think of a faster way of getting me there?" Captain Krill demanded, settling himself down in the chamber. "We have three minutes left to save this ship and everyone on it. Fire me, then follow me as best you can. That's an order!"

The black hole was so close that the penguins could see its dark and swirling heart through the windows. There was a creaking, groaning sound and a dull snap as the *Superduper Startrooper*'s huge tail fin snapped off. It spun past the windows and vanished into the black hole.

"Fire me, for plankton's sake!" Captain Krill roared.

Splash, Rocky and Fuzz turned the crossbow until it was facing in the right direction. Behind them, the vengeful robot chef was getting closer, shakily waving his remaining arm at them.

"DESTRUG! DESTRUG!"

"He's not so keen on tidying and cleaning any more, is he?" said Fuzz.

"One, two, three, FIRE!" shouted Splash.

Fing!

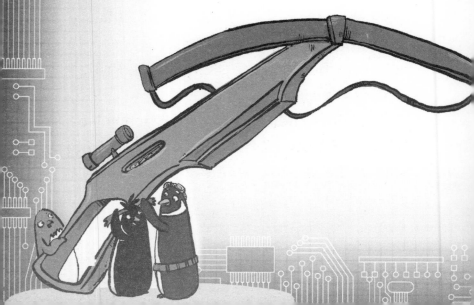

Captain Krill flew like a black and white arrow through the air, keeping his flippers by his sides and his beak as pointy as possible.

THUMP!

He skidded on the carpet, rolled beak over feet and smacked into the flight-deck door, which swung open.

A tiny orange alien was sitting gloomily on the pilot's chair with its chin in its tentacles. A huge pilot's hat was beside it, a pencil stuck in the hatband.

"Captain Krill of the *Tunafish*, reporting for duty, sir," said Captain Krill, getting to his feet.

The little alien gave a gloomy tentacled salute in return. "Commander Zizzwig Blap of the *Superduper Startrooper*. And it's madam."

"We need to turn your thrusters on," said Captain Krill.

Commander Blap waved a sad tentacle at a big red button way above Captain Krill's head. "Be my guest."

Fing!

"What a ride!" Fuzz said, jumping to his feet and dusting off his tummy. He waved cheerily at the pilot. "Hey, little guy, we're here to turn on your thrusters and get the hake out of here!"

"Like I just told your friend," said Commander Blap, "it's *madam*. And I can't reach the thruster button. *You* can't reach the thruster button. *No one can reach the thruster button.*"

"If we work together," said Captain Krill, "I'm sure we'll find a way."

Fing!

Rocky got to his feet and smoothed down his eyebrows. "Why aren't the thrusters on yet?"

"We have a problem," said Fuzz, and pointed up at the red button.

"That's not a problem," said Rocky. "That's a button."

The whole ship was groaning and creaking around them.

"Stand on my shoulders, Rocky," the Captain ordered. "Fuzz, you stand on Rocky's. See if we can reach it that way."

Rocky scrambled on to the Captain, pulling Fuzz up behind him. Fuzz stood on tiptoe, reaching with his tiny flippers for the button.

"Your friend is too small," Commander Blap said.

Fuzz's eyes sparked. He leaped from Rocky's shoulders and landed on the pilot's chair with his flippers raised. "You may be a girl," he warned, "but say the S-word again and I'll turn you into chowder."

Commander Blap stumbled backwards in fright, bumping into her hat and knocking the pencil out of the hatband. The pencil tumbled to the ground, missing the penguins by millimetres. The Captain looked down at it thoughtfully. It was almost as long as he was.

Fing!

"Good to see you, Splash," said Captain Krill, as Splash rolled through the engine-room door. He frowned. "How did you fire *yourself* down the corridor?"

"It was a simple matter of unravelling a loose thread from the carpet, tying it to the trigger, climbing into the crossbow chamber and pulling," said Splash.

"Now we have approximately one and a half minutes to get out of here. Why aren't the thrusters on yet?"

"Don't you start," said Commander Blap.

"I have a plan," said Captain Krill.

The penguins made a taller ladder this time, with Captain Krill on the bottom, then Splash, then Rocky. Fuzz balanced at the top, holding the pencil.

"That pencil's not too heavy, is it, Fuzz?" Captain Krill shouted.

"Nothing's too heavy for the Fuzzmeister!"

Fuzz did a little spin with the pencil in his flippers to prove it.

"ONE MINUTE!" Splash shouted.

It was difficult to hear themselves think, the *Superduper Startrooper* was shuddering so loudly. Reaching up, Fuzz leaned the tip of the pencil on the red thruster button – and pushed.

VVVVRRRROOOOOMMMMM!

They all felt the thrusters kick back into life beneath them. Lights flicked on. The flight-deck instruments winked and flickered and beeped.

"You did it!" said Commander Blap in astonishment. "You restored the power!"

"NOW who's small?" said Fuzz, as he slid back to the ground.

Clank. Clank. Clank.

What was left of Marin-8 stood in the engine-room door. His flickering eyes burned deep and red and vengeful.

"DESTRUG!" he crackled.

"We have no time for this," said Splash. "There's only twenty-five seconds left to turn the engines to full throttle!"

"Leave him to me," said Fuzz. "Ninja JAVELIN!"

He hurled the pencil.

PRANGGGG!

The pencil hit what was left of the robot chef's circuit board. There was a crackle of electricity, and a sigh, before Marin-8's eyes flickered into darkness.

"A loud Oomthrod hurrah for my pencil!" cheered Commander Blap, waving her tentacles with excitement.

"The pencil is indeed mightier than the sword," said Captain Krill.

"The pen," Splash corrected.

"The pencil is *totally* mightier than the pen," Rocky agreed. "Because you can rub stuff out."

"Is your missing tail fin going to be a problem, Commander?" said Rocky.

"Not at all," said Commander Blap. "It was only there for decoration."

"Ten seconds left. Where is the full-throttle button?" Splash said urgently.

"Next to the thruster button!" the Commander replied.

Captain Krill smoothed his ear patches. "Time to make the ladder again, team. Now, Fuzz, fetch me that pencil!"

CHAPTER TEN

A SUPERDUPER PARTY

Ten thousand light years away from the black hole, and the passengers aboard the *Superduper Startrooper* were back to their correct size and a party was in full swing. The ballroom was still in a terrible mess, but Hoovertrons were the last things any of the *Superduper Startrooper* passengers wanted to see just now. Besides, there weren't many left.

The Peabos had avoided the explosion and freed the other passengers from the library cupboard. Bright pink Jimjams and pale green Wardles were now taking turns at dancing their national dances of celebration, which both involved headstands and quite a lot of arm waving.

The huge Peabos towered over Fuzz as he ladled fresh green gazpacho into bowls.

"This soup's way better than the last batch," said the bigger Peabo. "What's in it?"

"I downloaded the top-secret recipe from Marin-8's circuit boards, cut the salt and added my own special touch," said Fuzz. "A handful of rainbow fish from what was left of the aquarium."

Splash was sitting in a corner of the dining hall, tinkering with a pile of robot wiring, while Rocky was in the middle, surrounded by a crowd of Ullabullas.

"So I climbed into the crossbow chamber, even though I knew it would probably mean my doom," Rocky was saying to his admirers.

Over on the dance floor, Captain Krill was looking as if someone had just bowled him over with a walrus.

"You!" he said to a four-legged alien in a bright red suit covered in glittering crystals. "You're Veezli Measly!"

The red-suited alien pushed his sunglasses up both noses. "I am."

Captain Krill's knees felt weak. "I'm your biggest fan," he said, holding out a flipper. "Captain Krill of the *Tunafish*."

Veezli Measly beamed. "I'm your biggest fan too. What was your name again?"

"Trustworthy Krill," the Captain gasped.

"Can I call you Trusty?" said Veezli Measly.

"Only if you want us to laugh for the rest of our lives, Mr Measly," said Fuzz, as he waddled past with two bowls of galactic gazpacho in his flippers.

"You're Veezli Measly," said Captain Krill again. "I can't believe you were aboard the *Superduper Startrooper* all along. You wrote my favourite song. You wrote 'Starstruck'!"

Veezli Measly winked and started singing: "*Starstruck, bad luck, being hit by a star can really suck...*"

"*Feet on fire, ears ablaze,*" Captain Krill sang back happily. "*Dazzled by your burning gaze...* It's a wonderful song, sir!"

"Please, call me Veezli," said Veezli Measly. He tapped Captain Krill on the belly. "If it hadn't been for you, Trusty, I would have succumbed to Marin-8's dastardly plan. I ran as fast as I could from the library when I realized I was shrinking."

Captain Krill looked at Veezli Measly's four feet. "They were your footprints in the coffee!" he gasped again. "Where did you run to?"

Veezli Measly patted his quiff. "The beauty parlour, of course, before I got rounded up with the others. If you are going to meet your end, you should do so looking as gorgeous as possible. If you had arrived any later, the universe would have lost my music forever."

Captain Krill clasped his flippers together to stop them shaking. "Thank haddock we reached the *Superduper Startrooper* in time to prevent such a tragedy."

"I'm going to write another song, Trusty," Veezli Measly said. "I shall sing about how you and your brave crew rescued me and all the other passengers aboard this cruiseliner from that terrible black hole. I think I'll call it 'Black Hole Battle'."

Captain Krill blushed again, even brighter than before. "You'll write a song about *us*?"

Veezli Measly was already humming and tapping three of his feet. "*Black Hole Battle, shake and rattle. It'll blow you all awaaaaay… Black Hole Battle, not just prattle, saved by penguins, yaaaay…* Yes, I like that."

"*Black Hole Battle,*" echoed the Wardles in booming bass voices, "*shake and rattle. It'll blow you all awaaaay…*"

"*Black Hole Battle,*" sang the Jimjams in high, bell-like voices, "*not just prattle, saved by penguins, yaaaay…*"

The whole room started dancing.

'They're dancing for you, Trusty," said Veezli Measly. And he winked.

It was Captain Krill's happiest moment ever.

P.S.

The *Tunafish* jetted away from the *Superduper Startrooper*. Completing missions was hungry work, so the penguins were having an early supper.

"Delicious rainbow-fish stew, Fuzz," said Captain Krill.

Fuzz narrowed his eyes at the Captain's plate. "You haven't finished it," he said.

Captain Krill hurriedly scraped up the last spoonful of stew.

"Whose turn is it to wash up?" said Rocky, resting his flippers on his full belly.

Splash smiled. "Marin-9 will do it."

Marin-9 looked almost the same as Marin-8, but instead of cleavers and whisks for hands, he had mops and brushes and polishing cloths. He stood quietly beside the table, his eyes flashing green.

"You've done a fine job reprogramming that robot, Splash," said Captain Krill.

"He looks as good as new."

"CLEAN. TIDY," said Marin-9 in a friendly voice. "PUT AWAY."

"Atta robot," said Splash, and patted Marin-9 on his shiny red back.

Lucy Courtenay has officially been
writing children's fiction since 1999,
and unofficially for a lot longer than that.
She has contributed to a number of series
for Stripes, including ANIMAL ANTICS.
In her spare time she sings with the
BBC Symphony Chorus and forages for
mushrooms, which her husband wisely
refuses to touch. If she were a penguin,
she would be a rockhopper. Her eyebrows
are already fairly awesome.